HUMS OF YESTERDAY

HUMS OF YESTERDAY

I STILL DREAM

Chandrabali Sen

EXCELLER BOOKS®
A GLOBAL PRESS

Hums of Yesterday
I still dream . . .

Paperback ISBN: 978-93-48892-95-9

First published in India in 2025 by Exceller Books,
An imprint of GE Group

Address: G1, Dream Apartment, Degree College Road, Belgharia,
Kolkata, 700056, India
www.excellerbooks.com

EXCELLER BOOKS®
A GLOBAL PRESS

Dedication

To my granddaughter Meghna, who lights up my life with the many colours of the rainbow.

Acknowledgement

I thank **Sabarna Roy**, without whose encouragement and help, this book would never have seen the light of day. **Saheli Mitra**, my editor, and her team at *Tales Talks Walks,* who designed the book—their valuable advice and constant efforts to present and lend shape to the book gave me a wall to lean on. I must also thank my family—my husband, **Pranabesh Chandra Sen**; my daughter, **Malini Sen**; and my son-in-law, **Aniruddha Sen**—for their support and encouragement. Lots of love for my granddaughter **Meghna Sen**, who gave me valuable time in reading and compiling my poems. **Devipriya Mukherjee**, a friend and author, read whatever I sent and inspired me to publish. Many thanks to **Madhu Banerjee** for sending Shillong photos for my book. I must thank the **Literary Committee of Calcutta Club** for publishing a few of my poems and the members who read them and encouraged me to keep on writing. Last but not the least, I would like to thank all my friends and relatives who read my poems, commented on them constructively, and motivated me to continue writing, as well as my publisher, **Exceller Books**.

– Testimonials –

Chandrabali Sen writes with the clarity of a person who has truly lived in the moment and with the veracity of someone who appreciates every experience that life has to offer. 'What If !' will stay with me for a long time. A book to return to often, especially if you are feeling restless.

Debdatta Dasgupta
Award Winning Book Blogger & Limca Book of Records Holder

Art is the expression of an artist. Chandrabali Sen is a spiritually elevated soul, who does not put up an act, nor express her fear, when there is no light around, but spots the dancing lace created by the street lights on her bedroom wall. She faces or goes through all the same challenges that life throws at us all the time, but doesn't miss a chance to spot the healing solutions within the very same problems. While we wait for spring she celebrates winter by noticing nuances that we fail to notice. If you want to explore an alternative perspective to the challenges, and experience the mundane or the dreaded, in the light of joy, then this inspiring work of art is highly recommended.

Abhijit (Tenny) Roy
Film Sound Designer & Sound Engineer

Chandrabali Sen's debut collection of poems, Hums of Yesterday pulses with visceral honesty, conveying emotional depth as well as personal insights. The narrative perspective is achingly sincere, born out of the mesh of memories and nostalgia; each line is a pathway to finding the future-self wading through a lifetime of experiences. Sen's cadence thrums with quiet urgency, transcending the quotidian to emerge as a voice that is vulnerable yet armoured with resolution.

Suchandra Roychowdhury
Author: The Shotgun Wedding (Aleph Book Company) Educationist, IBDP
English Literature (Singapore)

Chandrabali Sen writes from the heart and this helps her connect with her readers. Her poems are about nostalgia, vulnerability and pathos; and about acceptance, positivity and determination. She offers a much needed safe space which allows the reader to pause and reflect in the midst of a busy world; and emerge calmer and at peace.

Kalyan Karmakar
Food Writer, Columnist and Author of the Travelling Belly

“How dull it is to pause, to make an end,
To rust unburnish'd, not to shine in use! "

- Alfred, Lord Tennyson, Ulysses

Table of Contents

Foreword

In a world increasingly defined by haste and distraction, Chandrabali Sen's *Hums of Yesterday: I Still Dream* offers readers a rare sanctuary—a meditative journey through solitude, memory, nature, and the undying human spirit. This collection is much more than a compilation of poems; it is a tapestry woven from the delicate threads of a lifetime spent observing, feeling, and dreaming.

Chandrabali's poetry carries an authenticity that can only arise from a deep communion with life's varied seasons—of joy and melancholy, of hope and reflection, of youthful longing and the acceptance that comes with age. Whether she contemplates the golden hush of a twilight terrace, the irresistible pull of snow-clad peaks, or the tender ache of a memory revisited, her words pulse with a sincerity that touches the soul. There is both a quiet grandeur and an intimate immediacy in her verses: the grandeur of nature's immutable beauty and the immediacy of human emotions lived fully and honestly.

Organized thoughtfully into three thematic sections—Positive Reflections, Colours of Nature, and Introspective Musings—this book charts an inward and outward voyage. In the verses of *Let There Be Light,* Chandrabali embraces solitude not as a void but as a canvas for insight and gratitude. *Colours of Nature* bursts forth with vivid evocations of misty hills, dancing March winds, silvered moonlight, and the abiding magic of rain and sea. And in *Mirroring Life,* she turns her discerning gaze inward, exploring identity, resilience, the masks we wear, and the profound, often unspoken, yearnings of the heart.

What is most striking is Chandrabali's unwavering celebration of life, even in its twilight years. Age, she shows us, is not a curtain drawing to a close but an opening into new forms of wonder, reflection, and love. Her poems urge us to see beauty in the ephemeral, courage in vulnerability and hope in moments of stillness.

To read *Hums of Yesterday: I Still Dream* is to walk hand in hand with a voice that is wise, warm, and luminously human. Chandrabali Sen's poetic journey invites us to pause, to listen, and above all, to rise—again and again—with resilience, tenderness, and quiet grace.

Sabarna Roy
Author and Senior Engineering Professional
Kolkata
April 28, 2025

Preface

Age is just a number, and Poet Chandrabali Sen has proved that in real life, hanging on to the best moments that life could offer and tiding over the depressive ones through the magic of her words scripted as poems. *Hums of Yesterday* is not just another book of poetry and random thoughts. Rather, it encapsulates the journey of human life, from dreams to despair, from depression to joy, from outward to inward, from nature to soul and finally ends in hope and happiness. The book has been divided into three sections to give a direction to the poems as a collection of positive thoughts, natural elements and reflections of a keen and thoughtful mind.

Section I

Let There Be Light

This section of Chandrabali's poems carries the essence of solitude when a poetic soul enjoys the 'Me time' of the Twilight Years. At times, she is 'Alone' in her own space, but never 'Lonely.' She is a keen observer of her surroundings and thus includes the simple sights and sounds around in her poetry that elevate this section of her poems to a new height.

Reverie

I sink into my chair as twilight creeps in,
To enjoy solitude after a day full of din.
I don't switch on the lights but let the fancy roam,
And open my mind to fly away from home.
Yet all is not dark, for the street lamps are bright,
That bring to my room some semblance of light.
The breeze gently touches the trees in the lane,
Trespassing into my room through the open windowpane.
The leaves weave an intricate pattern of lace
That turns my bedroom into a heavenly place.
The shadows shiver and shimmer and gleam and dance
As I gaze at this artwork in a hypnotic trance.
My mind glides out onto a different plane,
Whose orbit carries me far—I don't feel the same.
The laws of gravity cease to exist
As I float high above, enveloped in a mist.
Is this death or sheer freedom? My pulse starts to drop...
Then the doorbell rings and brings my reverie to a stop.

Call of the Heart

What if we're past the prime of life?
Does the journey really end?
What if frailties curb our feet—
The road still twists and bends.

The heart still beats and bears and copes
With misery, loss, and pain,
Still thrills and feels and overcomes
The hurdles that remain.

The memories just come tumbling out
From hidden niches in the brain.
The snowy, golden mountaintops
Still beckon, call, and tempt.

What if we suddenly just break free
From the ties that overwhelm,
And follow that misty, lonesome road
That once we longed to tread?

The doubts and fears that bogged us down,
The things we left undone—
What if we dare to dream again,
Rejuvenated and recharged?

Melancholy

Melancholy, you are part of my existence.
You hover around and peep into my dreams.
You announce your arrival in my tears and sighs.
You break my heart while I smile and smile.
I open my arms and welcome you when no one is near—
When the wind is high in the trees, or there's a crescent moon in the sky,
Or in the scorching heat of summer, when the dust storms come,
Or a soft breeze caresses me with the scent of flowers.
You are mine alone; I share you with no one.
And when we are together, all barriers come down,
And I cling to you while my innermost thoughts
Come tumbling out from the deep, hidden recesses of my soul—
For you alone.

Solitude

Solitude, I met you unexpectedly last night,
When I went up to the terrace all alone.
There was no plan or design—just to view my favourite sight
Of the blue sky with wispy clouds, when the moon was full-blown.
The breeze was a whisper of delightful faraway places;
The moonlight heady, a kaleidoscope of shadow and light,
Making the familiar unfamiliar—a place of mystery and mazes,
And the concrete jungle was a fairyland when viewed from a height.
Solitude, I loved you unexpectedly that night,
Though you were a part of my journey right from the start.
Maybe it was the restlessness you soothed, or the magic moonlight,
But you charmed your way straight into my heart.

Sleepless

I am not sleepy yet,
Though the minutes tick and the seconds tock.
My eyes are not in drowsiness set,
Though time flies by through the hands of the clock.
I am not sleepy yet,
Though tomorrow has encroached on today.
The dark world outside looks strange
When viewed through the open window near my bed.
I try to tempt sleep by rearranging my pillows,
But sleep eludes, and thoughts interfere.
I am not sleepy yet, though the world is at rest.

Insight

The years roll by—slowly at first, then suddenly with speed—
Toward that ultimate moment, when they will take a giant leap
Into the darkness, that mystery none of us can know.
So, I decided to make a list.

The other day, when I looked in the mirror
And saw—not what I wished to see, but me as I really am—
The silver streaks in my hair, new wrinkles, the ravages wrought by time,
It was then that I wanted to make that list.
The ticking clock reminds me that I stand on the brink of an abyss.
When will it all end—swiftly or slowly?

There is not a moment to waste on wishful thinking or regrets;
Rather, use the time granted to make a new beginning—
Draw that bold, sweeping stroke that will remind others
That we, too, had loved and lived—not a mundane, routine existence,
But had achieved and created something worthwhile,
To leave behind as a gift for posterity, with love.

I make that list, cross it out, and write anew.
There are so many things that I still wish to do—
Climb mountains, trek and camp, dive and swim.
"All impossible dreams now," Time smiles relentlessly.
"Rather, do something befitting your age and capability."
But that ever-youthful heart within me rebels and says,
"Attempt the impossible; what does it matter if life is nearly at an end?"

Ageless Wonder

You're sad and sorry for your muscles ache,
Your grey and thinning hair is more than you can take.
Your memory lets you down and causes you pain,
And your bones — they break at the slightest strain.

Dear friend, it is time to pause and think
How the years have fled in just a wink.
And now we are sorry and full of care;
Things, quite clearly, are beyond repair.

A word of advice — please don't despair;
The gains and benefits of old age are rare.
For now, it is the time to sit back and relax —
No worries about deadlines or increasing tax.

You can tell that old rat race you're giving it a miss;
You'd rather give your spouse a hearty little kiss.
Your children are all grown up and achieving their goals;
Now they're your guardians — it's a reversal of roles.

We all have to pass through life's various stages;
No matter how we try, we can't turn the pages.
So just lie back in that favourite rocking chair,
And stop worrying about wrinkles and falling hair.

You've achieved what you could, and that is enough.
Now life is more easy, so don't make it tough.
There are many options — to garden or to tweet —
So, if you can't remember, Google will do it.

The Question & the Answer

The misty blue hills beckon—
"Come closer, come to us.
You were ours before the plains
Swept you away, remember?
You are a part of us;
We are a part of you forever.
We have your innocent childhood
And the soft beauty of your growing years.
Let the plains claim your summer and your autumn—
Whom will you choose in your winter years?
Do you ever yearn for lost tranquillity
And the smell of pines that rustle
Like silk through the velvet night?
It is not too late to return.
Sit still for a moment and think of us."

I remember, I do — every corner, every glen,
The dewy grass beneath my feet,
The full moon behind the eucalyptus,
The sweet peas, the church, the cones,
The bonfires in winter — all
Fresh memories, losing nothing to time.
You have my solitude and my silence,
My tears and the quiet smile
That lights up my face when I think of you.
Yet, it is not often that I do.
The pain of separation is too much.
Even now, I yearn, and I feel,
I miss, and I dream.
To return is not easy—strong bonds
Of a well-run home, comforts, habits,
Family and friends tie me down.
I will keep you in my heart
As a dream unrealised, a longing

That strains my bonds, and a
Temptation to be indulged in
When I am in melancholy.

Bliss

Life disappoints often, and hearts bleed.
Dreams unfulfilled and expectations shattered
Make you wish for oblivion, praying that you hadn't been born.
Yet, when a sudden fragrance is wafted by the breeze,
Bringing with it memories of innocent childhood or forgotten youth,
Or when the beauty of a blooming Amaltas stuns you into silence and bliss,
A sudden radiance descends on you,
And that elusive happiness and peace
Touch you for a moment—then disappear, and life goes on.

What If!

The evening advances stealthily as I settle down in my favourite chair,
To indulge in the pastime of wishful thinking by letting my thoughts fly—
Hoping, wishing, and wondering, "What if...?"
If I could still trek, I would walk through the undergrowth
And wade through gurgling streams to reach the Valley of Flowers.
If I could climb up the mountains or ski down snowy slopes,
In a flurry of snow, I would go there and race down.
I content myself with travel magazines, which invade my mind, thrill me,
Fill my heart and soul, and pull me inexorably onwards—
Past the concrete jungle into great heights and chilly air,
Always beckoning, carrying me towards the snowy mountaintops blazing in the sunlight.
And I smile to myself, "What if...?"

I find myself in a pathless zone, carving out a trail of my own.
The welcoming silence so deep that my very breath cuts through it.
The sudden call of an unknown bird breaks my trance.
I smell the spicy scent of wildflowers
And lose myself in the song of the swift-flowing stream.
I lie down beside it in my dreams and envelop myself in a world of sheer joy,
While pure contentment creeps into my soul — soothing, uplifting —
And I wonder in amazement, "What if...?"

I gaze at numerous tents at the end of the trail,
That suddenly widens into a green valley.
The hikers with jackets and sticks journeying into the unknown,
And a fierce desire, like that bolt of lightning streaking across

the sky,
Strikes my heart, and I long to be one of them—
Climbing up and down the gravelly slopes,
With a spring in my step and a song on my lips,
And the hypnotic spell of Nature's bounty all around me.
Suddenly, I feel as if I am transported there—blissful and at peace—
And all the "What ifs?" in my life disappear without a trace.

Remember Me?

When sudden darkness descends and lightning rips the sky,
The clouds hide the sun; thunder rolls and roars up high.
A storm invades my mind that seems to tear me apart,
As memories come swirling and tumbling from my heart.

I wonder, dear friend, if suddenly, in the night,
When the breeze is so shivery and the raindrops light,
Do you awaken like me with sadness and a sigh,
Or a feeling of loss and a tear in your eye?

In the season of autumn, when the rustling leaves
Fall and gather in a heap on the path beneath your feet,
Do you suddenly remember, with a gasp and a start,
Your longing for those moments from which you had to part?

Tell me, dear friend, that you remember still
How we gathered wildflowers on our treks up the hill,
And dropped down on soft grass in breathless delight,
As dewy cobwebs in the sun turned to diamonds so bright.

Do you stargaze even now in the deep, dark night
And stand frozen in awe at the exhilarating sight
Of twinkling gemstones that wink in the midnight blue sky,
That the colour of the ocean can challenge and defy?

Dear friend, do you still think about the thoughts that I do?
I send them flying through the air to fill your mind too.
Do you linger by the tinkling brook we found on our walks
And roam through the mists to sit on moss-covered rocks?

These memories and more of the bygone years
Often light up my life with joy and good cheer.
The tears are there too; I can't tell them apart—
They're all woven together in the fabric of my past.

Perfect Adieu

When do I wish to wave my final goodbye?
When I can no longer take pleasure in simple joys,
And the sight of a flowering tree, a glorious red sun,
A fragrant breeze, the green, green hill
Lose the power to make my heart leap with ecstasy.
When the rising moon ceases to weave its spell,
And the dark, dark night, with its myriad stars,
Sweeps me off no more to a land of fantasy.

When do I wish to bid adieu?
When the enthusiasm that drives me forsakes me,
And there is gloom and emptiness all around,
Yet I cannot fill my days by trying out something new—
The paint-a-little, read-for-hours, laugh-a-lot days are gone,
And there is no delight in making new friends.
When I am no longer a caregiver
But need help every step of the way.

When do I wish to enter that unknown orbit?
When the unconditional love in my heart dries up,
And I am angry and frustrated, and think that my age
Gives me the right to speak hurtful truths
And embarrass and pain others.
When I am tolerated or totally ignored
Because I have lost the power of interesting conversation.
When I live, but am no longer alive.

When do I wish to call it a day?
Before my loved ones think that I have lived too long.

Section II

Colours of Nature

This section of Chandrabali's poems carries the yearning of a nature lover. The poet is a big-time worshipper of natural beauty and touches upon the hues of seasons, the fragrance, colours and beauty that unravel before her eyes. Nature inspires her to write more, and her mutual bondage with the trees, birds, sky, clouds, etc, gets reflected in her words and opens a new vista in an age when conservation of nature is supreme in our minds and a necessity too for a greener world.

Hibernating in Winter

I smell the wood smoke in the air as I take a shortcut through the park—
Bonfires of fallen leaves from trees that now stand stark and bare.
A chilly whisper, the crunch of dried twigs underfoot,
And I am reminded that, at last, my longed-for season of Winter is here.

I wake up at dawn and stroll to the verandah
To catch that shivery breeze, the freshness in the air—
The misty morning, with the struggling sun peeping through—
As I sit browsing the newspaper, sipping my favourite brew.
Winter plays hide and seek and sends its tendrils far and wide,
Revealing its first steps with tiny signs for the sensitive mind.

I go back in time to the winters of my childhood
In the hills, all bundled up and warm—
The glowing fireplace, the oranges, the pine needles and cones,
The early morning walks with your nose so cold,
And flowers in a riot of colours,
Trampling over white frost spread thickly over grassy banks and lawns.

Many a time, Winter, I have found you enclosed in hibernation
On mountaintops up high.
I have chanced upon you in wondrous surprise
In the secret places where you lie,
While summer sizzles and rages all around in the dusty plains.
In Yumthang, you are a glacier and a carpet of snow
Among blossoming rhododendrons,
Which, in a blaze of colours, defy the cold,
While Rohtang and Sonmarg appear to be
The perpetual abodes of snow.

Here in the plains, where winter is short, mellow, and sweet,
I wait patiently each year to hear its stealthy steps—
To catch it at the start, to stretch out every second.
For though you are here now, you will soon disappear,
Whether slowly or in a sudden rush—and before I realise it,
Warm spring will give way to a sizzling summer.

Summer Rain

Suddenly, it came, with no warning at all—
Pitter-patter softly, the raindrops big and small.
Then, it broke with a roar over the city at noon,
Till the roads were a flowing stream all too soon.
Drumming on the rooftops and beating on the panes,
Rocking all the trees that border the lanes,
Lightning tore the sky and dazzled the eye;
The wind all around seemed to moan and sigh.
I gazed at the rainy sky, grim and grey,
And delighted in the rain as it fell all day.

March Wind

I stand by the window and feel
The rippling March wind hurl itself through the trees,
And sweep through my room as I clutch
At odds and ends whirling in the air.
All at once, in a flash—confusion and disarray—
The wild wind dancing around me everywhere,
A sense of freshness, freedom, instant happiness,
As I close my eyes and let the saucy breeze
Transport me to another time, another place:
A winding road bordered by swaying pines,
And the March wind sweeping through—
A sound like the dashing of the sea, a scent
So fragrant and spicy, your clothes all tangled,
Knots in your hair and tears in your eyes,
And the laughter of friends clinging to one another.

I open my eyes to a sense of loss, a pervading sadness
For the time that has passed—merciless, unkind—
Never to return, no matter how we yearn.
Oh, for those days of our childhood and youth,
When such simple things brought great joy,
And hope filled our hearts and overflowed.
That capacity for joy has long since fled.
Yet when the March wind blows, I remember,
And relive those days of innocence and bliss,
When dreams had wings and laughter rang true
Among pine forests in the sun-kissed hills.

Silver Moon

The moon is a sliver, a curved sickle,
Throwing just an aura of light,
So the tiny, twinkling stars have dared
To come out and beam tonight.
The clouds float by, soft and fleecy,
In white patches up on high.
The breeze is a shiver, a careless whisper—
Nostalgic, and makes you sigh.

The world never felt so sweet, so fresh.
Breathe it in; feel the magic around us—
Overwhelming in its promise of a better tomorrow,
When all impossible dreams will come to pass.

What does it matter if harsh reality
Intrudes when I wake up from sleep?
Something still remains—a touch, a shadow,
A whiff of bliss that our hearts will surely keep.

Sea Magic

The ocean captivates me and holds me by a chain;
Forever and ever, over me it will reign.
Shades of blue and shimmering green at times,
Or dashing with a roar, or moaning as if it pines.
An expanse of enchantment on a full moon night,
With the rise of the sun, it's a red and crimson sight.
The salty tang of the air, the spray flying high,
Rocking the boats gently, as on its breast they lie.
Fearful in a storm and awesome when it's calm,
With its sandy beach and waving palm,
Stretching on and on endlessly, as far as eyes can see —
From your fascinating spell, I shall never be free.

Ode to Distant Lands

I have left my footprints in your lands—
On the shores of your seas, in the sands.
Listen, and you will hear—a whisper, a sigh,
A gasp of enchantment that such beauty could lie
In the rolling moors, in highlands and dales,
In the swans that glide and the boats that sail.
I have left my heart behind in your quiet lanes and fallen leaves.
Oh, you foreign lands—you haunt my dreams!

My touch will linger in your flowers and trees,
A quick-drawn breath, a sense of wonder, a moment of peace
That captivates my soul, and all tensions cease.
Why do I feel that I'm an integral part of you?
My senses weave a web of strange déjà vu.
The wind in the trees, the fragrance in the air,
All whisper to me—they have a message to share:
"You're no newcomer to this foreign shore;
You've been here in your dreams many times before."

A Different Night

Will you walk up to the terrace with me?
It is a moonlit night when everything seems enchanting.
Yet, it is a different moon from the one I used to see,
Long ago in the hills, behind the shivering eucalyptus,
Peeping in and out through the leaves,
Playing hide and seek while I sat transfixed,
Throwing a cloak of molten silver over the valleys and hills,
And wrapping it all up in a veil of mysteriousness.

However, it is a different moon tonight—
More stark and vivid, bold in its beauty,
Without the shimmering softness I had seen before.
I long to go back in time to the moon I knew,
With its subtle light and tender hue.
Will you walk with me up the steps and through the door?
I will love this moon too, only, I need you by my side,
To chase away my sadness and hold me if I cry,
And tell me that though it is a different moon,
It is still a magical night.

Walk in the Rain

Walk in the rain with me, when the wind is blowing through my hair,
And the deodars bow down their heads, as if in prayer.

Walk in the rain with me. Don't speak—just hold my hand,
And all the thoughts you've thought for me, I will understand.

Walk in the rain with me, defying the thunder that roars up high,
When the lightning's a rapier of light, cutting a jagged tear in the sky.

Just feel the love that we share, and the pain and despair
Will vanish, as if they were never there.

Let us dream that you will always be there at my side,
And envelop me always—noon, day, and night.

That there is a forever where death doesn't play a part,
And love is as breath-taking as it had been at the start.

So walk in the rain with me, and blow the cobwebs from your mind.
Walk in the rain with me, and never, ever look behind.

Kerala, God's Own Country

You were there, ever-present, dominating my mind—
In my waking or dreaming moments, you I would always find.
But I feared that when I ventured into your shores,
Reality wouldn't match what I had dreamt of before.
I saw, gazed in rapture, and was totally enthralled
As, in a charming little houseboat, so slowly we crawled.
And Kerala became Venice as we cruised along
Through the myriad little waterways and islands so small.
The swaying coconut palms cast a hypnotic spell,
The dashing seas beyond seemed to heave and swell.
The white-crested waves on the edge of the bay
Dashed on the rocks, throwing up a fine spray.
The last rays of the sun on the blood-red sea—
The breeze was delightful, so wayward and free.

You have it all—mysterious forests, so dark and dim,
Bordering endless lakes whose shores they trim;
Rubber and spice farms and tea bushes so green,
Like a thick, lush carpet on the hillsides are seen.
Waterfalls rush down slopes, creating a perfect picture
That even jaded minds can easily enrapture.
A thousand strange birds breaking the silence of the air,
With their cadence creating a symphony so rare,
I could feel my heart brimming with ecstasy and bliss
When the first rays of the sun the hilltops did kiss.
I murmured a silent prayer of thanks and gratitude
For this vast and yet untouched emerald-green solitude—
Where man and nature form a bond so deep
That they promise each other to protect and keep
What exists in the midst of all this turmoil and strife:
A treasured place on earth that can be called Paradise.

Spectacular Kashmir

I am back in the nest; my long flight is over.
The holiday, eagerly awaited and honed to perfection—
Planned and mapped—is now a part of my memory,
Still fresh, still uplifting, still an amazement, and forever enchanting.
I talk about it, the scenery invading my dreams
All day and through the night.
I browse through the pictures, upload them;
However, nothing stills the longing in my heart—
The restlessness, the endless craving, and the pining
For that which I have left behind.

In the midst of daily chores, the gurgling rivers call.
The snow-capped peaks loom high in the distance.
Peeping in and out among the clouds,
A haven of escape from this blistering, sweating heat.
Always, those dark, mysterious woods beckon,
And the narrow path, winding through them, barely glimpsed,
Silently begs me to explore its depths.
How many times have I wished to defy
The demon of sightseeing—the rush of starting at dawn,
And returning, too drained out by too much beauty,
Crammed and stuffed into my head, so that
It becomes a jumbled mass and ceases to be pleasing.

I ask myself why I must always follow the path most travelled,
For I have longed to sit on the boulders by the river
And listen to its music as it sweeps by in eddies and whorls,
Or just gaze in awe at the snow-clad peaks,
Changing colour with the passing day,
While I relax on the lawn with a cup of fragrant Kahwa.
The verandah of the houseboat, bobbing with the waves,
The wide expanse of the lake, so peaceful and serene—
Why didn't I spend more time there, just sitting in silence,

Watching the shikaras float by like colourful birds,
Skimming the surface of the water?

Have I missed the essence of Kashmir
By rushing from place to place,
And, in the desire for more, gained less?
So, spectacular Kashmir, I must return to your fold—
To the blossoming apple trees and the sweeping slopes
Where sheep graze and shepherds watch,
The many shades of green and the towering firs,
Standing proud and tall, defying the snow-covered ground.
This time, I will see you in my own time and on my own terms.
I will follow my heart and find your soul.

An Ode to the Rains

The skies burst open, the rain came tumbling down,
First in drops, soon in sheets and rivulets, while thunder did frown.
Driven by the wind, the air was covered in a mist;
The trees on the roadside did sway and twist.
I stood by the window, watching the shower race,
Thrilled by the light spray the wind tossed in my face.
The road, a carefree river, a delight to behold,
While the wind screamed and moaned, and lightning rolled.
I longed to go to the terrace, for my heart was filled with zest,
For the rains called out to put my inhibitions to rest—
To welcome the sudden shower and get drenched in the rain;
My mind was made up—to stop me was in vain.
The coffee cup in my hand grew stale and cold,
In symphony with the downpour, so swift and bold.
As the real world retreated I was unable to blink,
I stood mesmerized and forgot to drink.
It was too good to last, as from my trance I awoke,
When the coffee cup slipped and shattered and broke.

The First Summer Rain

One looked at the sky in vain to hear the thunder roll,
To see rain soak the parched earth and the thirsty soul.
When hope was almost gone and the agony grew,
The skies opened up, and the rains came bursting through.
Surprise! Elation! A blessed sense of relief—
It was a dream, an illusion, was my immediate belief.
I put out my hand and let the raindrops fall,
And thanked the Almighty for this unexpected squall.

Delight

Welcome rain, most blessed rain, from up on high,
Sudden rain, oh pouring rain, you make me sigh.
Long-awaited rain through humid days and wakeful nights,
Now you're here, just racing down—a longed-for sight.
Darling rain, oh drumming rain, a feast for trees and crops,
Don't disappear till you fill my soul with your sweet, healing drops.

Andaman

The seas had lured me many times before,
So I thought that I knew what lay in store
For me, when I would visit Andaman—
It would be something that I had seen and done.
For surely, the blue sea that they all talked about
Was a non-existent myth—I didn't have a doubt.
I landed in Port Blair, and the sea was far away—
A glimmer, a shadow, maybe a bluish grey.
Then nearer it came as we moved towards the bay;
The dashing sea relentlessly threw up a fine spray.
And it was a heavenly blue, unbelievably true—
From where the colours came, I didn't have a clue.
As we gazed, it seemed as if buckets of green
Had been poured on the sea, and it looked aquamarine.
The colours merged together as if an artist was unsure,
For the greens streaked the blues, so neither was pure,
At the horizon it was deeper and closer to indigo—
Bands of green and blotches of blue,
Maybe mauve, azure, and turquoise too.
A thousand diamonds twinkled on the crests of the waves—
White sands, cool breeze, and all that one could crave.
And in that fading twilight, it dawned on me:
That a true blue sea existed to stun unbelievers like me.

Section III

Mirroring Life

How do you feel when you stand before the mirror of life? Do you see your own reflections or the mirage of unsettled dreams? Do you wear a mask, delving behind the veil to unearth? This section of Chandrabali's poems is more on the momentous reflections on life and the intrinsic introspective query that rocks every human mind: Who Am I?

Masks

Would you like to know me as I really am?
Why do I feel that it is something no one has done?
If you do, let us sit face to face in the dark,
Hold hands and talk, and I will let go
Of all my trappings, if you care to peel them off.
Try, delve deeper, and feel my pain—
What I value, what I love—and I will bare
My very soul, if you are up to the task.
Don't hesitate, for I long to be free
Of all the masks that sit so tight, one after another,
Such a perfect fit that I hardly know myself as I really am.
Years and years of trying to please, to conform, to adjust,
To fit into that special groove—a supple vine
Bending perfectly with the wind of public opinion,
Trying to be what you and others wanted me to be.

Why were you so content with me as I appeared to be?
My dreams, my thoughts, my fears were lying there,
Just below the surface, waiting to be released, shared,
Silently begging for a word, a look—
Crushed under the weight of despair and wanting,
Yet afraid to take that first bold step,
Afraid of your lack of interest and need
To know that hidden me who is buried deep.

The Real Me

I do not know the real me, the one who makes me whole,
For a thousand different beings pop in and out from the core of my soul.
I can spy a tireless homemaker, a painter, a bookworm, a cook,
Loving wife, mother, and granny—wherever I look.
One who can spend lazy hours just dreaming in the dark,
A poet longing to express herself, just waiting for that spark.
There's a stargazer somewhere deep inside who can let her thoughts fly,
Yet, at times, I spot a stranger who is inhibited and shy.
I curl up in a corner to wait and watch and see,
But I fail to grasp and fathom who is the real me.

She suddenly appears when I'm unprepared,
When I'm filled with fear that I ever dared
To stand up and fight with my back to the wall,
When I'd gladly give up and go back and crawl.
She is my inner strength, my wisdom—the best part of me,
Yet I can't pin her down; she's so elusive, you see.
She emerges in a crisis and then waltzes away,
And smiles at my futile attempts to get her to stay.
She is the source of my restlessness, my wants and needs—
And the answer too, to all of these.

A Woman Basically

A phenomenal woman I try to be,
But in the attempt, fail miserably.

When I delve deep inside,
Here's what I find —
Some tenderness, some care,
Some doubts I can't share,
A softness, a need
For love which is deep,
Some pain, some despair,
Some wounds beyond repair.

This is the real me —
No phenomenon, but
A woman, basically.

I try to achieve so many things;
I set myself deadlines to give my feet wings.

But when I dig deep inside,
Here's what I find:
A faltering, some fears,
Some trembling, some tears,
Guilt that still lasts
For failings in the past,
A shyness I can't shed,
Inhibitions that I dread.

This is the real me —
No phenomenon, but
A woman, basically.

Being Me

When everything conspires around me
And makes me a target for all,
In spite of the lies that spin a web,
The hurtful jibes, the spiteful words,
I will be me.

I won't let a sarcastic word escape my lips
Or take pleasure in giving pain.
I will only deal in kindness and truth
And give the love in my heart free rein.
I will be me.

You can call me a doormat if you will,
But it keeps my soul at peace.
For when I say a cruel word
Or twist a tale to suit my ends,
Something inside me bleeds.

I would rather meet the barbs that fly
And cry alone in the dead of night,
But the bliss that fills me, the joy that thrills me
When I don't retaliate or give in to hate,
Is beyond compare.

You can call me a coward if you will,
But I just can't bear to be rude,
Or say smart things to make others feel small,
Or laugh at their failings to win applause,
I will be me.

You can call me stupid if you will
And think I don't grasp what you really mean—
When I do, but prefer to hide it from view,
For though you try to make me a copy of you,
I would rather be me.

Just Bear with Me

Forgive me if I should ever ask to have what I may not,
To wish for something that cannot be.
When yearnings and desires churn a riot in me,
Remember, it will only last a while.
So, please bear with me.

When the twilight's golden glow casts its spell
And the air a lingering fragrance brings,
If I long to talk about sweet, inconsequential things—
That one forgets soon after but remembers the warmth they give—
Please, bear with me.

When, in the background of the dark, velvety night,
The stars blink back tears and shed a soft, subtle light,
And I long for you to be there by my side,
Maybe hold my hand for just a little while,
Please, bear with me.

In the midst of the workload of a busy day,
When I spy the flaming Gulmohar bursting forth in vivid colours,
And stop by to stare and admire,
Letting the world and its worries go on,
Please, bear with me.

When my thoughts drift and fly on a windy winter night
And I gaze at the pale, shadowy moon and sigh,
If I am distracted and unmindful, and tears blur my eye,
Don't think I lack contentment or the love that I had—
Just bear with me.

Secret to Happiness

When you're feeling really low for no reason or rhyme,
When you're bored and jaded and down in the dumps,
When you're sad and sorry and feel like giving up,
Remember, there is still more to life—
So, cheer up.

Go stand by a window and watch
The play of sunlight on the leaves of trees.
And when the wayward breeze caresses your face,
Think that life is still sweet—
And cling on.

Call up a friend, write, or read,
Or do something else instead—
Something you've never done—
And think that life is still a lot of fun—
And walk on.

When nothing goes right and there's no end in sight,
Think of that rainbow or that moon-drenched night,
Of the friends you cherish for their attitude to life,
And your heart will tell you there is something more
To be gleaned from life.

Dilemma

There are so many options that I don't know what to do,
How to choose some over others—I haven't got a clue.
What to include and what to leave out,
Decisions must be wise and without any doubt.

Should I go out into the garden and watch a flower bloom,
Or drown myself in music while sitting in the gloom?
Will it be internet—mail or Facebook? The choices make it hard,
Or a cup of coffee, all alone, while I let down my guard.

It's been a week since I've touched a book;
Some picture albums deserve a look.
The full moon night just weaves its spell—there's magic everywhere,
Some for you and some for me, and there's enough to spare.
An azure sky and white floating clouds make it a tempting sight,
But time is slowly creeping by while I am in a plight.

Basket of Surprises!

Isn't it enough to have lived each day
To the best of our capabilities —
Smiling and making others smile,
Making a difference, however small,
Touching others and being touched in turn,
Feeling blessed at the sight of
The changing colours of the sky, the flight of birds,
Thrilling to the soft breeze wafting through the leaves,
Or being drenched by that sudden surprise shower?

Isn't it enough each morning to wake up to a new day,
Filled with promises—the gift of time granted—
To repair our mistakes, to forgive, to forget,
Knowing we are surrounded by dear ones,
To love and be loved, interact and bond with friends,
To sip that cup of steaming tea,
Do little everyday things that never lose appeal,
And give our hearts that short burst of bliss?

Isn't it enough each day just to wait
For the surprises that life may bring?

Introspection

It is not as if I have never wished
That I should make another start,
And wipe past failures and begin again,
With new goals and hope in my heart.

But then I look back and think again—
Something's been achieved, and it's not been in vain.
It has left an imprint in the core of my soul,
And its healing touch has made me whole.

When I try to remember the special dreams, so sweet,
That I've dreamt—but now they seem to retreat—
I can't tell them apart; they flash by so fast,
Interwoven, interconnected, a part of my past.

But you stand out in my journey through life,
A support, a comfort in my times of strife,
When you stood by my side, so silent and still,
And I could lean on you on my treks uphill.

You add new meaning to my life
By just being the way that you are.
The things that you do—and those that you don't—
Make the sadness in me disappear.

Life's Moments

This is what life is all about—
The sudden memory that arises
From the depths of the subconscious
To bring a smile or a teardrop,
When standing by the window
You catch a glimpse of the sky, layered in shades of grey,
Promising imminent rain.

Life is all about small moments, sudden surprises,
More about little spells of joy and bursts of bliss.
In spite of pain and sorrow, life is about spying that rainbow at the end of a trail,
When the cloud curtain pulls back to reveal that snowy magnitude,
Turned golden by the setting sun.

Life is about finding that wildflower, that butterfly, that rare fern,
When a long-awaited bud blooms,
And reveals an ethereal beauty and fragrance.
Life is about that kind word, that thoughtful act,
The attempt to bring out a smile on the face of a weary soul—
About acceptance, gratitude, and awe.

Life is about unconditional love, for the loving heart is happiest.
It is more about giving than receiving,
And, at the autumn of life, that glow in your heart
Tells you that your life has been well lived.

Tell Me Now

Tell me now, don't wait till another dawn—
All that you've thought and dreamt from night till morn.
Tell me now, all that you didn't say;
Make a start—don't wait till another day.
Tell me now; it's never a moment too soon.
Tell me now, before the waning of the moon.
Look up and see the myriad stars blink;
Now is the time to tell me what you think.
Tell me all that you'll feel when I am gone—
How, without me, you'll be all forlorn.
Tell me now, before it's too late to share;
Show me now that you'll always care.
Don't wait for that perfect moment to arrive;
It may suddenly steal by, no matter how we strive.
There is no moment like the present, for we all know—
Even though we cling, life is all about letting go.
So, hold me now and open your heart;
Tell me now, before it's time to part.

Depression

I am surrounded on all sides by an impenetrable wall.
No escape for me—this stifling atmosphere
Suffocates me, gags me, makes me feel so small
That I want to cry till I can shed not another tear.
This blind, aimless search for a way out,
Those moments of agony that shatter my peace,
When my heart is breaking and I am filled with doubt
That all my troubles will ever cease.
Where is God's mercy that the sages glorify?
Am I unfit even to receive a drop?
With His help, I can all storms defy
And at a harbour of calm, make a stop.

Someday

Someday, I will not let my steaming cup of tea get cold.
Someday, I will put all my activities on hold.
If I wish to linger in bed after a restless night, I will,
Or get up at the crack of dawn before the sun lights up the windowsill.

There are so many days and so many hours in a year
To give of myself to those I hold most dear.
Surely, I can savour a whiff of freedom with a contented sigh
And stop all the clocks and bid time goodbye.

That cosy verandah, where the plants grow without much care
And spread large leaves to create a haven rich and rare —
There I will sit back with my cup of tea
And whisper to them in peace and tranquillity.

The phone may ring or the doorbell buzz —
That's an everyday annoyance; that's all it does.
The songbirds will trill and capture my heart;
I may glimpse an unknown bird streak by like a dart.

Someday, I will not hurry or rush to get things done;
That will be another day when the race must be run.
A day is all I claim to do as I dare;
The years have flown by — there's not much to spare.
So, let me get started on this journey of delight;
A day is all I need for this miraculous flight.

Reflection

What are my pleasures of sight?
A bird in the sky, soaring to its height,
A blooming bud, half hidden by a leaf,
The dashing sea against the reef,
The full moon rising in a star-spangled sky—
I could watch all these until I die.
The whispering palms, the shimmering sands,
Faces gay with laughter and waving hands,
Rain falling in torrents, puddles in the streets,
Two men fishing in a bush full of reeds.
Snow-capped mountains and green grass lawns,
A river full of gliding swans,
A winding road bordered by trees,
Children running in playful sprees,
A turquoise-blue sky, white fleecy clouds,
A thick fog covering the town like a shroud—
These I delight in, these I love to see,
Richer than all treasures they are to me.

When I Am No More

When I pass away into eternity,
And my existence is a thing of the past,
Don't despair at the awesome futility
That nothing will ever last.

A summer even glistening with stars,
Will whisper my message to you.
A beautiful garden, blooming with flowers,
Will revive my memories anew.

Perchance your eyes will be dimmed by tears,
And my absence may drown you with pain,
The lifetime ahead may fill you with fears
That there only misery will reign.

See my face in the heart of a rose,
My voice in the whispering pines.
The rosy colours when day draws to a close
Will bring back a picture of mine.

I shall live on in Nature, ever by your side,
Though you feel I have left you alone.
So laugh and be happy; take life in your stride,
Till death claims you and makes you my own.

9 789348 892959

Printed at Repro India Ltd.